Pip and Posy

The Scary Monster

Axel Scheffler

 nosy crow

It was a rainy day and Posy
was a little bit bored.

She decided to do some cooking.

In the kitchen, Posy put on her apron and washed her hands.

First, she took out

the sugar   the butter

the flour and the eggs.

Then she stirred everything together.

She plopped the mixture
into the paper cases.

Then she put the tin
into the oven.

Careful, Posy.
It's hot!

Posy was waiting for the cakes
to bake when she heard a tap
at the window.

It was a big, **furry** hand!

Posy felt a little bit scared.
Whose hand was it?

Next, there was a knock on the door!

"Grrr!" said a voice.

Posy was very scared indeed.

The door opened. It was a monster!
"RAAAAA!" said the monster.

Posy started to cry.

Oh dear!

The monster came right
into the house.

But then Posy looked at the monster's feet.
She stopped crying.

"Hello, Pip,"
she said.

"Hello, Posy," said Pip.
"I'm sorry if I scared you.

Would *you* like to be
a monster now?"

Posy put on the costume.

"Raaa!" said Posy.
Pip laughed.

Pip and Posy went out into the garden

and played until tea-time.

Then they had a glass of milk,
and lots of cakes!

Hooray!